The Heart of Leo

by

Blythe Ayne

BOOKS & AUDIO BY BLYTHE AYNE

Fiction:
The Darling Undesirables Series:
The Heart of Leo - short story prequel
The Darling Undesirables
Moons Rising
The Inventor's Clone
Heart's Quest

Nonfiction:
Love Is The Answer
45 Ways To Excellent Life
Finding Your Path, Engaging Your Purpose
Horn of Plenty—The Cornucopia of Your Life
Life Flows on the River of Love
How to Save Your Life Series:
Save Your Life With The Power Of pH Balance
Save Your Life With The Phenomenal Lemon
Save Your Life with Stupendous Spices

Short Story Collections:
5 Minute Stories
Lovely Frights for Lonely Nights

Children's Illustrated Books:
The Rat Who Didn't Like Rats
The Rat Who Didn't Like Christmas

Poetry:
Home & the Surrounding Territory

CD:
The Power of pH Balance —
Dr. Blythe Ayne Interviews Steven Acuff

The Heart of Leo

by

Blythe Ayne

The Heart of Leo
Blythe Ayne

Emerson & Tilman, Publishers
129 Pendleton Way #55
Washougal, WA 98671

All Rights Reserved

No part of this publication may be reproduced, distributed,
or transmitted in any form, or by any means, including
photocopying, recording, or other electronic or
mechanical methods, without the prior
written permission of the author, except
brief quotations in critical reviews and
other noncommercial uses permitted
by copyright law.
This is a work of fiction.
Names, characters, places, and incidents are fictional.

Book, cover design & first graphic by Blythe Ayne
Other interior graphics thanks to NASA

The Heart of Leo
Copyright © 2016 Blythe Ayne

Prequel to *The Darling Undesirables* series

www.TheDarlingUndesirables.BlytheAyne.com

www.BlytheAyne.com

Paperback ISBN: 978-1-947151-21-5

[1. FICTION/Magical Realism
2. FICTION/Science Fiction/Steampunk
3. FICTION/Fantasy/Urban] I. Title.
BIC: FM

First Edition

DEDICATION

*For Anyone Who has Ever
Wished Upon a Star*

The Visitor

Heart lay on her narrow bed under the geodesic Star Dome, excitement tripping her every synapse. *Tonight!* Tonight the Leonid meteor shower would be the most brilliant in thirty-five years—last seen long before her fifteen years!—when Comet Tempel-Tuttle would make a dramatic and rare outburst, sparkling across the sky.

The three-dimensional, super-telescope geodesic dome inset in the ceiling of her room at the Darling Undesirables Facility was a gift she'd received years before when she told a news reporter her favorite thing was stars. Star gifts poured in from everywhere, addressed simply "To: Heart"—the most adored of the Darling Undesirables.

The window, connected to a satellite external to Earth's atmosphere, ran on dark energy. Thus, the geodesic shapes of the window functioned as an active star map to the constellations.

Heart propped pillows behind her head and stretched out, waiting for the meteor shower while contemplating her favorite, though faint and remote, star, deep in the heart of the great constellation, Leo. Caffau's star, one of the oldest known, and most anomalous stars in the Universe.

The brilliant furnace of the first massive, unimaginably hot and fast-burning stars after the Big Bang forged hydrogen, helium, and a dash of lithium into carbon, oxygen and iron. But Caffau's star, hanging around for 13 billion years with the oldest of stars, was composed of hydrogen and helium, but no carbon, no oxygen. *No lithium!* Very strange ....

Amidst Heart's contemplations, the Leo star shower began. Brought near by the star dome's magnification, it appeared to sparkle and fall all about her. Delicate pastels and hues shot through with bright golden streaks like celestial, massive lightning, fell about her room. It was more than she'd hoped for, more than she could have imagined, though she'd seen many meteor showers.

But as she reveled in the cosmic light show, she noted a brilliant, pulsing pastel light in the center of the shower that seemed to be heading straight for her little geodesic dome window. The strange light was not shooting or falling or behaving in any way like the other lights of the meteor shower. And another peculiar thing about it was—it seemed to be coming from

Caffau's star, faint and far away as it was. Heart had the star dome centered on Caffau's star, and this *light* remained centered on it.

The mysterious light grew brighter and larger, while the meteor shower faded, the flashing streaks of light trailed faintly. But this shifting-yet-steady, pastel luminescence continued to flow directly toward the center of Heart's geodesic star dome. It became so brilliant, that Heart shielded her eyes. She considered leaping from her bed, but the fascination of this light pinned her, unmoving, peering around her forearm to see if the impossible brightness continued to move through impossible eons of light years toward her.

And it did.

Suddenly, the light rested upon the geodesic dome, pouring over it like a pastel, molten metal.

Heart imagined herself discovered in the morning by the Keepers, turned into a pastel metal art object, stretched out on her bed, arms reaching toward her Star Dome.

Perhaps not so terrible.

Closing her eyes while she braced herself for the tempered glass to shatter, she heard, instead a soft, *"splink!"*

Opening her eyes, the dome above had returned the view of the dark and peaceful night sky. But Heart became aware of an aura in the room. Slowly she turned to take in a vision neither she—nor anyone else, she was fairly certain—could be prepared for.

A glimmering, pastel Being slowly took form in the center of her room.

Oddly calm and unafraid, Heart watched as the Light continued taking on shape. Arms, legs, head, finally settling into a fluxing, pulsing, pastel pearlescence. Though without facial features—at least, not any Heart could discern through the light, she felt the Being smiling at her.

"Ahh ... hello?" Heart whispered, slowly shifting to sit against the wall, then crossing her legs.

The sound of delicate wind chimes sparkled around the room. "Hello."

"You ... you ... can ... talk."

"Indeed, I can talk," the many chimes answered.

"Oh!" Heart whispered, "your voice! It's like your light."

"Your voice is like your light, as well," the Light Being answered.

"*My* light!?"

"Yes." The Being's pearlescent torso became mirror-like. There, Heart saw a different light, swirling with colors in paisley forms, stirring with delicate animation. Heart watched, fascinated, the amazing light. She began to see her own eyes among the moving light formation. Then her face became defined.

"Oh!" Heart jumped up from the bed and moved away from the mirror image. The Light Being's appearance has not frightened her. But this reflection of herself as a stunning Being of Light was too much!

"No need to fear, Little Star. See your beauty!"

"*No*, I'm not beautiful! I'm a Darling Undesirable—a misfit, a broken, incomplete being."

"Though you're unique among your kind, your beauty is equal to your rarity. Be calm, my child. All is well."

As the Light Being's chimes trilled, Heart watched the reflection of her Light fade. She wasn't sure if it was the sound of the many-chimed voice, or the disappearance of her reflection, that calmed her more. She became awash with a sense of peace, and, yes, an emotion she had to think for a moment to name, as she had rare occasion to feel it—joy. *JOY!*

"Joy," she whispered softly.

The Light Being nodded. "Pure, absolute joy, sweet Heart. Yes."

"One could do anything, feeling such an emotion! Create, pray, heal ... or even ... think nothing ...."

"True."

Heart returned to the edge of the bed, passing through the Light Being's aura as she did so. It tingled like the chimes. "*Ahh!*" she sighed, letting the feeling pour through her. "Extraordinary!"

"Extraordinary. And yet, ordinary," the Light Being said.

"Not for me."

"Soon you will change."

What did the Light Being mean? Why had the Light Being come here? To her? A small, incomplete human, an error in experimentation. Living in the lap of luxury, but only because of humanity's guilt for causing her—and her kind—to come into being in the first place.

"Ah, Little Star, such thoughts! You are neither incomplete nor an error. Your existence is no mistake!"

Shocked and annoyed, Heart muttered, "I must watch what I think, if you're going to read my mind without warning."

"I apologize. I ought to have told you, your thoughts have the same volume, or are actually a bit louder, than when you speak vocally."

Heart shrugged. "Anything is possible, I guess, with an entity from Leo's meteor shower. But—why would you say I'm not a mistake?"

"Because you're not, because you are so far from a mistake. You have been *intended.*"

"Intended! Who—who 'intended' me?"

"Father Inventor."

"Father Inventor? No. He's too ... too ... *majestic* to bother with anyone like me. Least of all me, a freak without a heart. What use could I possibly be to his amazing work?"

"All will be revealed in time, dear Heart." The Being's Light shifted to violet and purple, then settled on the floor, "But first, let's chat."

"*Uhm*, okay." Heart moved to sit on the floor, facing the softly pulsing light. "I wouldn't know how to disagree with you, even if I wanted to."

The chimes jingled sweetly. A little chuckle, Heart decided.

"First, let me recap my madness," Heart said. "A meteor from a shower breaks loose, comes rocketing through my Star Dome, then starts a conversation. And I listen. As if it's real."

"I'm not from the meteor shower. I used the meteor shower to get your attention. I'm from what you know as Caffau's star."

Heart jumped up in agitation. "Oh, yet crazier. *Caffau's star!* You're saying you're from Caffau's star. The very star, in the entire universe, with all the billions and billions of stars, *the very star! I've been studying.*" A fear began to overtake Heart as the thought took form that her mind *must be slipping.*

Was it not bad enough to have been given life in a test tube without a heart? Did she now have to lose the one thing she believed she had?—a fairly good mind?

"You're not losing your mind, Little Star. I've been telepathically letting you know I would visit. That's why you've had an interest in Caffau's star."

"Again," Heart argued, "not possible. I watched you come in under minute. Caffau's star is 4,000 light-years away."

"True. I came on the Interstellar Dark Energy Highway."

Heart raised her eyebrows. "I'm sure. Four-thousand lightyears in a minute. We have Dark Energy Highways, and it takes several hours to circle the globe."

"That's because of two things. One, humans are new in their understanding and use of Dark Energy and, two, Father Inventor knows enough about human avarice to hold back on the full potential of Dark Energy he has, so far, harnessed."

"You came from Caffau's star, through the Leonid meteor shower on a Dark Energy Highway, 4,000 light-years away, just to sit chatting with an insignificant 15-year-old girl on a remote and insignificant planet."

The palest of lavender light reached out, from the Light Being and, with the delicate touch of butter-fly wings—brushed against her face. Heart relaxed into the light, and the noisy bee buzzing in her brain became quiet. "Not exactly. I came to show the girl—decidedly not insignificant—on a distant, yet beloved planet, some celestial phenomena, essential teachings, which she will soon need."

Heart sighed deeply. "But. Why. Me? Why? *Why me?*"

"I must teach you many things. More than that, I cannot say at present. Just—trust me."

"Trust you! I don't even trust myself at the moment."

"I know. You have reason for caution. But for now, I ask you to throw caution to the winds."

"And if I do?"

"I'll show you."

ꝶo Place Like ꝶome

The Light Being rose, colors charging up and changing, swirling through its body. "Shall we go?" Its many chimes voice asked, while arms of Light opened wide. "You must come willingly, of your own accord."

Heart wanted to ask where they were going—*and, yet, she didn't want to ask.* She wanted to go wherever this Light would go, she wanted to hear forever the adorable, compelling, many-chimes voice.

Did it matter where the Light Being took her? Anywhere would be better than here, in the sad, dreary, stifling, luxury prison of the Darling Undesirables Facility at Long Prairie. *Anything!* If this was a crazy-real dream, well then, let it be a crazy-real dream, and enjoy it to its fullest.

And if she was losing her mind, nothing would stop it. So, again, she might as well enjoy the crumbling of her synapses. She thought of the really, really sad Darling Undesirables, the broken little human-forms with very little mind. But they seemed contented enough. *There might be something to not having to think about everything.*

And, last, but decidedly not least .... *WHAT IF THIS WAS REAL?* What if this was—*really truly!*—a Being from Caffau's star, who was about to take her ... somewhere?

She'd go anywhere the Light Being wanted to take her.

She stepped willingly into the Light.

"Beautiful!" the chimes rang out. They whooshed up, right through the Star Dome and out into the deep, dark, peaceful, night sky.

"Are you taking me to your home? Are you taking me to Caffau's star? If I leave Earth's atmosphere, shouldn't I be wearing a protective suit? And a means to breathe?" This is not a very good dream, she told herself, I'm not even providing the essentials.

"I'm not taking you to Caffau's star. And no, you needn't worry about a space suit."

Heart felt a shift in the flow around them, and sensed they had left Earth's atmosphere. She turned to look back at Earth. *Oh! So gorgeous!* Through the rainbow of the Light Being's colors, Earth glowed.

Not an insignificant little planet! So beautiful, it almost hurt to look. Heart felt like crying, she became so overwhelmed at the sight, the globe of her home, huge around them, its sparkling blues and greens of land and water, its misty white clouds, even now, receding as the Light Being zoomed away from Earth.

"How ... how utterly, inexplicably painfully, beautiful!" Heart sighed.

"Yes. Like any treasured jewel. Small, but so precious."

"Even if you took me back to my room this very minute, I am changed forever. I'll never be the same, just from this few moment's sight. I've looked at many planets in my nightly Star Dome explorations, but, really, nothing is quite like Earth."

"You're right, Little Star. Nothing is quite like Earth."

"Where are you taking me?"

"Look just up ahead ...."

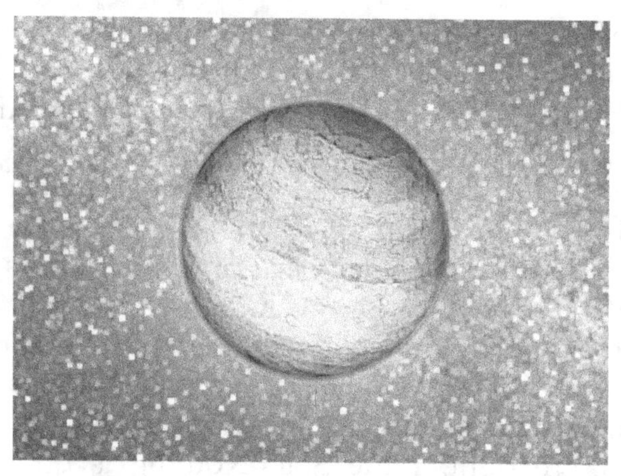

A Lonely Planet without a Star

Moments later, the Light Being paused. Everywhere there hung darkness.

"There, you see?"

In the middle distance, Heart faintly saw what appeared to be a planet—floating alone in empty space. No sun to warm it, no other planets for companions. "Lonely Planet!"

"Yes. The planet you've been watching for some time. A baby among planets, born only 12 million years ago. Wandering through space all on its own, quite content not to be attached to any solar system."

"*Ohhh!*" Heart sighed. "When I first found this planet ... I thought ... I felt ...."

"I know. It seemed like this planet, 80 lightyears away, was like you—floating through space, alone."

"That's right. I thought it was just like me. I have no family, Lonely Planet has no family. I float through my life with no one having any clue what really is going on inside me. Except my best friend, of course. Except for Eye. But Lonely Planet doesn't even have a best friend. Sad."

"Not true, dear Heart. Lonely Planet has you. In its singular and great mind, it feels your thoughts, and your feelings on those nights when you reach out to it, feeling lonely. You are great company."

"*Hmmm* ... my few years of thinking about it must be a very small blip on its 12 million years."

"Before you came along, it had no particular emotions. But when you brought to it your loneliness, and your companionship, you woke it up—it started to feel. In fact, it's contemplating manifesting some children on its surface. Of course, since it's very cold, they would be different from Earth's children. But you, Heart, have inspired Lonely Planet to consider the companionship of children upon its surface."

"Is that ... good?"

"I would say it's very good. Consciousness is the evolution of all being-ness. Becoming aware, and then creating. Moving forward into consciousness and awareness is the action of love. Which, of course, is the underpinning of the Creative Force. The energy of love, of adoration, of focus. Care. Expanding the self into ever greater Being."

"I see," Heart said, feeling her love of Lonely Planet. "I hope that Lonely Planet has, one day, beautiful children. And I really, really hope its children treat it with the love and respect it deserves."

"Yes, this is the desire of all planets that have manifested children. Earth is magnificent, with its myriad amazing life forms. Oh, the beauty of the creatures and plants. Quite appreciated throughout the Universe."

"*Hmmm ....*" Heart sighed.

"What is going through your mind, Little Star?"

"I think you know ... I'm thinking about how it seemed like I had this bond with Lonely Planet, how we are the same, floating around, utterly alone. But I wasn't as alone when I sent love to Lonely Planet. And now, I see that's because love was being sent back to me.

"And I've been so, so sad, because it seemed to me that every Darling Undesirable is a lonely planet. But ... if Lonely Planet feels the love I send it ... maybe, I mean, just maybe, the love I feel for each broken Darling Undesirable—maybe it touches them too ...."

The Light Being's chimes rang and sang softly about Heart. "Precisely true, dear Heart. And the second important lesson I mean for you to learn this night."

"The second? What's the first?"

"*Hmmmm ....*" The Light Being sighed thoughtfully, "you tell me."

"Well ... oh!"

"Yes?"

"I'm shy to say it."

"But you must. You must more than say it. You must affirm it."

"Well, then ... you have shown me that I am not insignificant. The rush of insight I had looking at my beautiful home, Earth, hanging, suspended in the midst of the great unknown, so sweetly and so beautiful. Knowing that's my home! Stunning and precious. And how ... how fortunate I am to live there.

Even if I'm a Darling Undesirable. Even if there are many problems, even if humanity is so many kinds of messed up, we are surrounded by beauty. Just that moment is worth everything. Everything bad or sad. Because no amount of bad or sad comes anywhere near to touching my awe."

The Light Being wrapped its arms of light even closer round Heart. She felt warm and whole, as she had never experienced before. *"Little Star,"* the Light Being whispered softly.

They paused, hovering, communing with Lonely Planet, then finally the Light Being said, "Say good-by to Lonely Planet for now, and let us visit other wonders."

Heart closed her eyes and sent Lonely Planet a kiss across the distance. As she opened her eyes, she saw it flare and felt a warmth on her cheek. "Did that really happen? Did Lonely Planet kiss me?"

"Of course!" The Light Being's chimes trilled and chirped.

Heart touched her still-warm cheek. *To be kissed by a planet!*

Anomalous Nebula

Safe in the Light Being's arms, Heart sailed away from Lonely Planet. They returned to the Dark Energy Cosmic Highway, and before long, they were suspended before a nebula that had captured Heart's attention ever since she first saw it years before.

"*Oh!* The Red Square Nebula! A dying star that produces this totally improbable light," Heart said.

"Yes, it's quite stunning."

"It's not natural, being square. Natural objects are curved. Only artificial objects have corners. But—*Look!* Four corners! I read a theory that it's emitting gas in two cones at a ninety degree angle from Earth. But here we are, far out in space, and still it's a beautiful red square.

The ancient Native Americans used to weave talismans they called 'God's Eye,' that looked like that. Maybe it's an advanced civilization building a Dyson sphere. Or maybe, from what you say, it's the intelligence of the star itself, producing this beauty."

"Some things are more meaningful in their mystery, and so I'll leave you to contemplate that as you will, Heart. But, do you see how everything has it's place ... no matter how anomalous. In truth, the anomaly is the beauty. You, dear Heart, are not broken or incomplete. You're a child of the universe, part of the perfect plan. Unique. Your actions in your future will ripple out far beyond even your lovely planet."

Heart shook her head. "I don't understand. But right at this moment, I don't want to understand. I just want you to show me the wonders of the Universe, as if we're wandering through Keeper A's garden, while we contemplate the flowers of the Universe, that's enough for me."

"Excellent—then let us visit another celestial flower."

The Very Strange Object

The Light Being swirled around and turned an enormous celestial corner.

"Hanny's Voorwerp!" Heart breathed as a vast green glow came into view. "*Look!* From here, the black hole is clearly visible. The theory is that a small galaxy passed by that big spiral galaxy and pulled out a tidal tail of gas as it passed. Then a black hole at the center of the galaxy turned on a quasar that happens to shine on the tidal tail. So when gas pouring out from the black hole crashes into the tidal tail, *stars form!*"

18 - The Heart of Leo

"Quite spectacular," the Light Being agreed.

"So spectacular, so amazing," Heart agreed. "One morning while stirring cream into my tea, I saw this very same thing. There was a large blob of cream, and a little blob of cream—the little blob got caught up in the edge of the big blob's swirl, and, rather than being absorbed, it pulled the edge of the big blob away, spiraling off to the corner of my cup.

"I said, '*Hanny's Voorwerp!*' out loud, right at the breakfast table. Of course everyone just looked at me. Well, I'm strange even among the strange."

"You have your own dynamic power, even if you're a smaller galaxy."

"*Hmmm. Perhaps.* Is this another lesson?"

"*Hmmm. Perhaps,*" The Light Being chuckled with its honeyed chimes.

"Unfortunately, my tea didn't start to make stars. Wouldn't that have been something? But then, how could I possibly drink down a cup of stars?"

"Would have been thrilling."

"I'd be a true star child then."

"You *are* a star child."

"I am? Am I? You keep calling me Little Star."

"You are a true star child. Everyone is made of the stuff of stars."

Heart considered the Light Being's comment. "That's true. Every physical thing is made of star dust, star light, star energy. *Every. Thing.*"

"Let's get closer to the baby stars."

"Let's!"

The Light Being carried Heart among the forming baby stars.

Lightness and joy engulfed Heart, and she laughed out loud. "So much happiness!"

"The joy of Becoming. The joy of Being. You know the joy of Being."

"I'm feeling it now, but I've only felt pure joy with Eye, and, even at that, only rarely, as I worry about him so much."

"You needn't worry about your friend, Heart. Eye is in my care. And he has a destiny of his own."

"How is that possible, when he has no eyes? He needs me. Eye's destiny and mine are entirely wrapped up in one another."

"Your destinies are involved, but that needn't mean ... well, let's just leave your future to your future. It will unfold in due time."

"A future without Eye? No, I cannot imagine it."

"As I say, time will tell its own story. But for the moment, let us take a peek at another celestial wonder."

"Sure—as long as we're here."

The Light Being chimed in amusement. "Yes, as long as we're here!"

A Glorious Ghost Nebula

"*T*aurus!" Heart exclaimed as the constellation came into view.

"Taurus. What do you love about Taurus?"

"Ira's Ghost Nebula, more formally, the, 'Infrared Astronomical Satellite'—IRAS Ghost Nebula. Although small in the vast scale of things, this is one of my favorite mysterious celestial wonders."

"Why is that, Little Star?"

"Because of the strange bright light. It's just cosmic dust, but it has a brilliant chevron of light—from nowhere. Maybe a young star crashed through the gas and star dust, traveling at 200,000 miles per hour, through the nebula and out into space. Maybe it left behind it this arrow of light, beaming through eons upon eons, from—just—dust! It makes me think that, no matter how insignificant something, or *someone* might be, they can still shine a light. Once given light, they can shine that light. It becomes their own light. They can share it."

"Like you."

"*Oh!* I don't know about me. But, if whatever light I capture from studying, from listening, from being open and curious—if I can share that light, it would be wonderful. And if I can share the light of love, even if I'm not sure what love is ...."

"You know what love is—in the first few moments of meeting Eye, you knew Love. Love is strong and healthy in the garden of your mind."

Heart listened intently. Wonderful words, like nothing she'd ever heard! No one at the Darling Undesirables Facilities talked about love in a real way. Heart had only ever heard people talk about love being in their heart. And since she didn't have one ....

"What thoughts!" the Light Being exclaimed. Love does not reside in a physical spot! Love is everywhere."

"Yes," Heart breathed, "I want to believe that."

"Believe it," the Light Being said. "What you feel, here and now for this ghostly nebula, shadowed star dust and nearly invisible gasses, *even this!* is love."

"I'll accept that. And ... I love you, too. All that you're showing me—how could I not love you?" Heart looked up into the Light where eyes would be, if the Light Being had facial features. *But wait!* There, like bright stars, glowed eyes, benevolently, deeply, compassionately looking into her very depths.

"You have eyes!" she exclaimed simply.

"I do."

"But—why didn't I see your eyes when you first came into my room?"

"Simply seeing my light was almost more than you could handle."

"But I can handle it now. You've flown me all about the Universe—it does seem as though I ought to be able to handle some facial features!"

With that, the Light Being's entire face lit up in all its beautiful glory, while the chiming voice exhaled a laugh that reached all the way to Ira's Ghost Nebula, making it undulate softly like a curtain in a breeze.

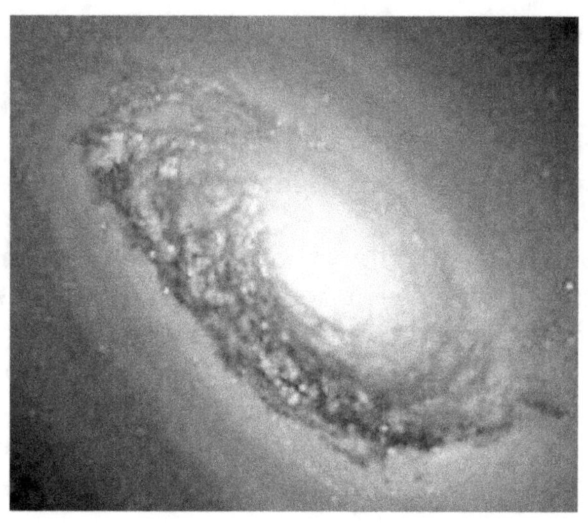

Sleeping Beauty

Heart didn't want to tell the Light Being that she suddenly felt exhausted and sleepy, even in the midst of her joy, love, and excitement.

But the Light Being responded to her thought. "I know, Little Star. It's a lot. I will take you to one more of your favorite galaxies, and then, back to your little bed."

"I ... I wish I wasn't tired. It's quite strange. I can go days without sleep. I don't know anyone who can stay awake like I can. But I think I've never, never, *ever* felt so exhausted!"

"It's more than simple exhaustion, Little Star. You're reprogramming. Down to your most minute cells, you're rewriting who you are. You're rewriting your future."

The Light Being stopped its billowing movement. "Here is the perfect celestial wonder to conclude our journey this night."

Heart looked to the panorama beyond.

"Sleeping Beauty! A very strange galaxy—but *beautiful!* A contrary galaxy, literally contrary. As a rule, stellar gasses rotate with the stars in a galaxy. But in the beautiful but strange Sleeping Beauty galaxy, the gasses close in rotate with the stars, but from 3,000 to 40,000 light years they rotate counter-wise to the stars. *So strange!* Freakish."

"Freakishly beautiful," the Light Being said.

Heart nodded, sensing the massive rotation and counter rotation, even if it could not be seen, she felt the peculiar magnetism. "Yes ... freakishly beautiful!"

"And another metaphor in which you see yourself."

"Yes, wise Being of Light, you see through me again. In my strange galaxy on Earth, I appear to rotate with all the sad, broken little stars around me. But, really most of me is whirling completely opposite to those around me. Alone in my own orbit. Alone."

"Not alone, Heart. Never alone."

"Heart nodded, her head falling upon the shoulder of Light, while sleep, or more like sheer unconsciousness, overtook her. "Not ... a-l-o-n-e ...."

The next thing she knew, the Light Being gently laid her on her little bed, and pulled her blanket up around her. She looked at the Light Being, now delicately translucent. She could see the Star Dome through its shifting pastel lights.

"I ... Love ...."

"I Love, too," the many chimes said more softly than tiny rain drops on baby rose petals.

"*Wait!*" Heart jumped up, wide awake. "Where are you going to sleep? Where will you be when I wake up? What will our tomorrow be like?"

"Relax." The Light Being stroked Heart's hair, and she felt sleep overcome her again. "I am going back to Leo, to Caffau's star. And ... tomorrow, you will not remember anything from tonight."

"*I'll remember!* Of course I'll remember!"

"No. You'll not remember a single thing. But all the understanding you gained tonight of yourself ... that will remain. You won't seem different to anyone. But you will to yourself. You will know yourself in a different way. You've rewritten your internal cosmic code, and you'll have a new bravery. It will surprise you on occasion. Nothing can stop you now."

"*I will not forget you!* I love you. You showed me that I *can* love! That I *do* love. How could I love you and forget you?"

"Just another one of the Universe's strange anomalies. Loving deeply, and not knowing why. It's good. It's better than good. Sleep now, Little Star, and forget."

"*I ... won't ... forget ....*" Heart whispered as she fell into deep, impossibly deep, dreams of stars.

But, immediately, she forgot. All the memories of traveling the cosmic Dark Energy highway locked away in the recessed vault, far below conscious thought and knowing.

But ... *right on the surface of feeling.*

PostScript:
Heart's story, in **The Darling Undesirables,** is quite different from the night she spent with the *Light Being.* But much of who she discovered herself to be was revealed that night, while sealed from her memory, yet impressed upon her DNA, into her farthest reaches.

The Darling Undesirables picks up in the world she lives in. The one she is destined to change.

Following is the first chapter of **The Darling Undesirables ....**

Chapter 1

Heart stood in front of The Museum of Scientific Improbabilities and Unpredictable Oddities. She looked up at the sable brown stone building, up and up she peered, until her eyes came to the lights of the Mechanical Aurora Borealis, pouring extraordinary, revolving images into the sky.

"My Darling Undesirables," Keeper D said, "this is a great and glorious privilege you've been given by Father Inventor. Please show your appreciation."

The small band of Darling Undesirables stood at quiet attention, without a clue what was expected of them. All of them, that is, except Heart, peeved by Keeper D's pseudo-pious act for the benefit of people streaming past them into the museum.

Keeper D folded her hands as if in silent prayer. The Darling Undesirables imitated her gesture. But Eye didn't and Heart didn't. Eye didn't because he couldn't see. Heart didn't because whatever she believed, it was private.

People poured around them on both sides, keeping a respectful distance while sneaking sidelong glances at Heart. Her fury rose.

She had eyes. She had ears. She had hands and arms and legs and feet. She had hair and a mouth. In short, she looked like an ordinary girl of eleven or twelve, although she'd recently turned fifteen.

There was the staring with sidelong glances at her, and the blatant staring when they saw Eye. He'd become the most famous Darling Undesirable. He had no eyes. No residual eyes. No eye sockets. No suggestion of eyes. His face was soft skin from forehead to cheek to chin, with a beautifully formed nose and mouth.

Heart saw Keeper D glimpse at her out of the corner of her eye. Quick as snake tongues, she reached out and grabbed Heart's hands, clasped them together to her chest, then returned to her own position.

Heart tried to move her hands, but, strangely, a magnetic force held them gripped to her chest. As she gazed at the roiling lights in the sky above, the delicate pastel colors spun into a ball and became an intense, heavenly purple, forming an arch. Filmy pale green haloed out from the purple arch. Heart sensed a tugging at her entire body, as if she would pull up and soar right through that arch, five hundred feet above the ground.

Everyone around her stopped, stunned and mesmerized, watching the path that formed in the sky. Heart's feet tingled, she felt light, certain she was about to leave the ground. Keeper D grabbed her hands and pulled them apart.

"That's enough from you, Little Miss!" she hissed.

The lights of the Mechanical Aurora Borealis coalesced back to their calm patterns. Slowly people came out of their spellbound state and continued to file into the museum.

Stunned, shaken, weak, Heart stumbled. Keeper D caught her. "Whoopsie!" she said loud enough for those nearby to hear, grabbing Heart's collar. "A little dizzy from all that looking up, are we?"

She grabbed Eye's forearm with her other hand, then shuffled all the Darling Undesirables forward. "Let us see the wonders within," she exclaimed, a smile glued onto her features.

"What happened?" Eye whispered to Heart.

"I ... I'm not sure."

"Hush," Keeper D warned.

"I'll tell you later."

"There's nothing to tell," Keeper D said under her breath, "except more attention-getting from our little heartless wonder."

"Oh!" Heart exclaimed, but kept her retort to herself.

Keeper D's sad band of young charges came up to a jovial man at the middle entrance, while everyone else flowed through large doors on either side. Although the Darling Undesirables never paid for anything, they must always have their identity chips scanned.

"Wasn't that amazing?" The cheerful doorman said to Keeper D as he clicked each child's wrist implant—except, of course, Arms, whose identity chip was in his neck.

Heart watched Keeper D's smile fade, knowing how she loathed entering into conversation, especially pleasant chat. "What?" she replied brusquely.

"The Mechanical Aurora Borealis. I've never seen it do that. I've been here since The Museum of Scientific Improbabilities and Unpredictable Oddities opened, and I've never see that."

Keeper D shrugged. "I didn't notice anything—I was attending to my Darling Undesirables."

The doorman nodded, subdued by Keeper D's unpleasantness.

"Where do the lights come from?" Heart asked.

Keeper D gave her a warning look. Heart ignored her.

"Well, my little Darling, we do not know."

"What are you trying to tell her?" Keeper D argued. "They come from the museum."

"No, Miss Keeper, indeed, they do not. As I say, we don't know where they come from. In the sky. Somewhere. Somehow. There is a mechanism that produces the aurora. I've watched the lights for years. Sometimes I've been fortunate enough to see truly beauteous forms—but I've never seen them do anything like what they just did. Opening up like that, making an arch, showing a path. Amazing! I wanted to walk on that path ...."

"Me too," Heart said, nodding. "I felt ...."

"You were not addressed," Keeper D extended Heart's wrist under the identity device.

The jovial man clicked Heart's wrist, lowered his head and looked at her from under his brows, then winked at her. She felt herself grinning—as if her mouth would stretch right off her face. No one had ever winked at her!

"Have fun in The Museum of Scientific Improbabilities and Unpredictable Oddities," he said, turning her hand over and giving it a pat.

Keeper D's hand went from Heart's collar to the back of her neck, giving it a squeeze, not quite painful, but definitely an unspoken, "Don't speak!"

Heart tried to wink back at the doorman, but having never seen anyone wink before, she blinked both eyes. The doorman chuckled. Keeper D's grip increased. Heart didn't care. She and the doorman shared a secret moment. Keeper D could do nothing about it.

Heart would never, never forget this moment.

Something continued to shift in her. It had started with the light path that opened in the sky and continued through to this moment when a gentle man had really, truly looked at her. Had really, truly seen her. Not staring at her because she was a Darling Undesirable, but looked at her because—*because she was herself.*

She'd be content to go home right now, having seen and felt more joy and happiness in ten minutes than altogether before in her life—other than, of course, her time with Eye.

Inside, the Darling Undesirables had gathered in a tight knot, waiting for Keeper D. Heart saw a round little woman with a round face, big round eyes, a little round button of a nose and a round happy smile hurrying up to them, moving gracefully as if her feet were on rollers.

"Sorry, sorry to be late, *sorry*. The change in the Mechanical Aurora Borealis has everyone aflutter. A group in the star gazer room was completely agog. *Such* a unique display! Did you see it?" The round woman nodded cheerily at each of the children in turn.

"Some did, and some didn't." Keeper D's frown deepened. "However, I fail to understand this big fuss over a mechanical light show."

"Oh!" The round woman's round smile turned to puzzlement. "It's a very big deal. It's a very big deal," she repeated, as if she couldn't believe she'd had to say it the first time. "I mean—do you not know your prophecy?"

"Prophecy? Oh no. No. Stop right there. The children are not to hear that. We at the Darling Undesirables Facility at Long Prairie do not believe in such things. And—and," Keeper D was clearly brought to her absolute wit's end, "and this is a *science* museum. This is *science*."

"Oh dear," the little museum docent said, clearly distressed. "I'm sorry to have upset you. I shall rephrase my talk." The round "O" of her smile returned to her face. "I'm so fortunate to be the docent chosen to show you around today. I'm pleased to meet our special little Darlings, Heart and Eye." Her eyes squinted down into half moons of delight.

Heart looked up at Keeper D, who rolled her eyes as if the docent's sweetness was too saccharine to endure. "Let us move forward, shall we?" she said flatly.

"Yes, yes, of course. We're going to have so much fun today!" The docent took Heart's hand, pulling her away from Keeper D's grip.

Heart reached out and grabbed Eye's hand, and the three of them led the Darling Undesirables from the Facility of Long Prairie on their tour of The Museum of Scientific Improbabilities and Unpredictable Oddities.

This day just gets more and more remarkable, Heart thought, giving Eye's hand a squeeze.

"You happy?" he whispered.

"More than ever."

"Wow!" he breathed.

"I wish you could see ... well, everything. But most especially, the lights in the sky."

"The lights in the sky," he repeated. "You'll show me—later. Tonight."

"Oh yes. I'll show you tonight. And tomorrow and tomorrow and tomorrow, until you beg me to stop." She would show him the amazing Mechanical Aurora Borealis when they were alone tonight, just like she showed him everything in the world, and all the things she made up not in the world. With words, words, words. All the pent up words she stored every day from the Keepers "shushing" her.

She would relive the lights, she would relive her feeling. She would relive how her feet tingled, and her body became light and pulled toward the Mechanical Aurora Borealis. She would tell him, and she would tell herself again and again, too, so that she'd never forget, how the Mechanical Aurora Borealis had surely responded when she clasped her hands over her chest. Strange coincidence.

But wait!

"Eye, you had your hands clasped, did you feel it?"

"Feel what?"

"The lights—the pull of the lights."

"Lights can pull? You've never said that lights can pull."

"They can't. I mean, they don't, usually. But, did you feel a pull?"

"No. I don't think so. I'm not sure I understand."

For a fleeting moment, Heart let herself feel a thrill of selfish exuberance. The strange pull must have been for her. If *anyone* was going to feel something, it would be Eye, whose sense of feeling substituted for vision. "Don't worry. I'll explain—tonight."

"Be quiet!" Keeper D hissed, coming up to Heart, Eye, and the docent, herding the rest of the Darling Undesirables, each clinging to a fat golden rope strung along the aisles of the museum for them to hold onto.

The docent, who had begun a brief overview of the hall they were about to explore, clapped her mouth shut at Keeper D's command.

"Not *you*," Keeper D said, only marginally civil. "I mean that one." She pointed at Heart.

"Oh!" The docent exclaimed. "I didn't hear her. Was she talking?"

"All the time."

"I'm telling Eye what I'm seeing." Heart dared to speak. They were in public. Keeper D was the only Keeper here. Heart thrilled at the opportunity to say what she always wanted to say. It wasn't *precisely* accurate that she was describing the surroundings to Eye at that moment, but she was about to, and she wanted to be able to tell him what she saw without Keeper D constantly *shushing* her.

"I think it's truly sweet of you to share with him what you see." The little round woman gave Keeper D a disapproving look, which Keeper D returned with double interest upon it. The docent shrank back a step.

"It would be *truly sweet*," Keeper D said with an edge of sarcasm, "if she'd stay in the realm of the real world. It's tiresome having to reteach the poor little guy, after she's filled his head with ridiculous untruths."

The docent raised her eyebrows almost into her hairline. "I can't believe it! Look how sweet she is. And she holds onto Eye's hand most conscientiously."

"All an act." Keeper D leveled her gaze at Heart, daring her to speak.

Heart felt tight in her head like she did when she became extremely upset. She returned a defiant look. "It. Is. *Not*. An. Act. And you know it. You know Eye is my only friend. *You're* the actor. The First Directive is that Keepers love us—*and you do not even like us!*"

Almost all of the Darling Undesirables gasped, even the ones who had a hard time understanding anything.

The docent's hand became sweaty in Heart's hand. "Oh dear," she muttered. "And I was *so* looking forward to today."

Heart broke her stare-down with Keeper D. She knew she'd pay for her outburst for ever as long as she lived at the Darling Undesirables Facility at Long Prairie. Eye held her hand tightly, not making a sound or moving a muscle. Heart let her gaze fall to the plaid of her shirt sleeve. Brown-over, beige-under, dark green over-over, pale green under-over-under. She could hear Keeper D's voice, but only as a far away buzzing.

"Great. Just go into a fugue state. Fine, while the rest of us have some fun." Her voice faded as she and the Darling Undesirables—all but Heart and Eye—went down the hall.

Seconds later the cheery little docent's face blocked her view of the plaid. She had kneeled down on the floor in front of Heart. She stroked Heart's arm, where she tried to stay with the traveling plaid. "Are you all right, honey? Are you okay?"

Heart wanted to answer, but she couldn't talk while she was in the plaid.

"She follows the map in the plaid," she heard Eye say. She wanted to smile. He made a good student. He couldn't even see, had no idea what "plaid" was, but he understood what it was like for her when she went there.

"I see," The docent said. "So—she's all right?"

"Sure. She'll come back out in a minute. You're sure nice. What do you look like?"

The docent giggled. "Oh my goodness! How does one describe oneself? I'm round. I have a round face. I smile a lot. I have a tiny little nose and big round eyes. People think—because I'm very friendly and because I'm sweet and caring—that I'm kind of slow. There seems to be a weird idea that if you're smart, you must be snotty and rude. But I'm actually quite intelligent and nice. I know a lot more than I let on.

"For instance, and I suppose I should't tell you this—I researched your group, and I knew who was coming. I know quite a lot about each of you little Darlings. I also researched your Keepers C and D and E. I know Keepers C and D are not very nice, and Keeper E is not very attentive. I was sort of prepared for anything to happen today. But not what the Mechanical Aurora Borealis did. No I wasn't prepared for that. Someone in your group has some kind of powerful energy.

"I only saw the lights change and do something unusual once before, and that was when ...."

"I felt it pulling on me," Heart said, finally unweaving from the plaid.

"Did you?" The docent turned to Eye. "Did you feel it pulling on you, too?" The docent asked Eye.

"No. I don't understand what Heart means when she says she felt it pull."

"Magnetic," Heart said. "Like I was a magnet, and it was a magnet. Strong, I thought my feet would leave the ground."

"Very, very interesting." The docent nodded, then stood. "I supposed we'd better catch up with your group. Try to stay out from under Keeper D's radar, okay, my darling Heart?"

Heart nodded. "Okay. I don't know what's gotten into me! And I'm sorry I made you sad. I like your round smile very much."

"Thank you, sweet thing. But you didn't actually make me unhappy. It was a bit of an act on my part."

"Oh!" Heart exclaimed. "Why?"

"For this very reason. I had hoped to be able to chat with the two of you without her big ears."

Eye giggled. "Keeper Big Ears!" He whispered.

Heart and the docent giggled too. *"Shush! Shush!* You two, you'll get me in trouble if you repeat that!"

"It's our secret," Heart said, kissing her index and middle fingers audibly and raising them.

"Our secret," Eye said, kissing his fingers and raising them. They locked fingers. "Miss Round Face is our particular excellent friend."

"Yes. All words between us remain secret."

"All words secret," Eye intoned.

"Well, I'm flattered. That's a fascinating ritual you have."

"Thank you," Heart said shyly. "We have a book's worth of 'secret rituals.' We have to at that crazy place we live."

"Hmmm ...." the docent took Heart's hand.

They wandered down the empty hall completely by themselves. As the Darling Undesirables explored, museum guards went ahead, clearing out other patrons and roping off each wing in turn with fat golden ropes.

Their footsteps clicked against the marble floors, echoing off the glass cases.

"Marble," Eye said. "Different kinds. Are there mosaics in the floor?"

"Yes! There are beautiful mosaics in the floor. You can 'see' the floor by the sound?" The docent asked.

"Sort of. But I can't see the images."

"Clever, clever child. Ah, here we are."

The three of them came up to the Darling Undesirables, who stood, not moving, gathered around Keeper D.

"Here we are," the docent said again, gaily. "Eye asked an important question. He could hear the different types of marble as we walked on them, and, clever boy that he is, asked if there are mosaics. He's right, the museum has beautiful marble art embedded in the floors in every wing, made of the finest marble to be found anywhere."

The docent moved to the middle of the group. "Each wing of The Museum of Scientific Improbabilities and Unpredictable Oddities has marble mosaics in the floor that depict the types of items housed in that wing."

She gestured to the floor where they stood, "We are in the wing that explores what life would be like if the inventions using electricity had become our main means of energy. In the floor in this wing are the images of gigantic poles stuck in the ground, with wires strung from pole to pole." She swept her hand in arcs, imitating the marble electric lines in the artwork under their feet.

Then she shuffled the group over to a showcase. "In these showcases, you will see many examples of numerous failed experiments attempting to get electricity to work universally.

"Inventors had come up with devices that they called 'telephones' for communication, fragile glass bulbs that sparked electricity to make lights, and heaters that used electricity to blow heat through homes." As she talked, the docent led the children from glass case to glass case, pointing to examples of the curious inventions.

"Even Father Inventor dabbled in electricity for a

while. The biggest problem with electricity was that everyone shared this means of power. Everyone had to be on what was proposed as a 'grid.' So, if there was a problem with the grid, everyone would be without power—no lights, no heat, no communication, no cooking."

A couple of the children who were following the docent's talk gasped. Keeper D "tsked" as though the mere thought of the system was ridiculous.

"But everyone would have power most of the time?" Heart asked, her attention drawn to a charming little house, not quite as tall as she, demonstrating what a household run by electricity would be like. A little girl sitting in a rocking chair read by a yellow light. It looked cozy.

"That was the theory," the docent said.

Heart had heard of electricity, but she hadn't known of its many useful inventions. She thought about the people in The Periphery, living without power, in poverty and darkness. "But—couldn't the people who live in The Periphery use these inventions? This 'grid' of power, even if it quit sometimes, would be better than the way they're living now, with no power, wouldn't it?"

The docent exchanged a quick glance with Keeper D. Heart saw Keeper D frown and shake her head with a small, but extremely emphatic "No!"

"Well," the docent said slowly, thoughtfully, nodding at Heart, "I guess I've never really thought about it in that way. It's certainly an interesting idea. A very interesting idea," she mused, moving down the hall. Heart could see that the docent utterly wished she could get away from Keeper D. But that would not happen until the tour of the Darling Undesirables in The Museum of Scientific Improbabilities and Unpredictable Oddities was over.

Heart scurried ahead to come alongside the docent, even abandoning Eye. "But what ....?"

She glanced at Heart out of the corner of her eye with a look that said, "not now!" And then she winked at her. Too! Just like the doorman. Heart wished and wished she could share this remarkable secret code with Eye.

But, it could never be.

Keeper D came up to them with the rest of the Darling Undesirables in tow. "We don't even need to think about electricity," she exclaimed as if there was a raging argument. "Ever since Father Inventor harnessed Dark Energy, we have more power than we can use. Electricity—*pah!*"

"If that's true," Heart argued, "why don't the people in The Periphery have power? Why do they live in darkness and cold? Dark Energy must not be enough for everyone."

"Oh—you are *so exasperating!*" Keeper D said, her voice grinding in a quiet, simmering anger.

"I don't care if I am. I just don't want those people to be in the cold and dark, and hungry too. I saw the children, huddling together at night in darkness on my 3-D. That's wrong!"

Keeper D sighed, clearly resigned. "I will tell you. Those people are being punished."

"Bun-ished?" Heart asked. She looked at the docent, who looked away.

"Punished," Keeper D corrected. "P-u-n-i-s-h-e-d," she spelled.

"What is 'punished?'" Heart looked at the other Darling Undesirables. They were getting bored. Some had wandered a few feet away. Some were putting their hands on the glass of the showcases, which Heart knew Keeper D would never permit. So this subject was very big, to completely take Keeper D's mind.

"When you do wrong, you get punished. The people in The Periphery have been sent out of the cities. They are exiled from our Dark Energy advantages. They have a difficult life because they have hurt society. They have hurt others, and they cannot live with those of us who live in harmony, and who care for one another."

Heart, who had just said that Keeper D did not care about the Darling Undesirables, wondered what things the people living in The Periphery could possible have done that were even worse than how Keeper D was all the time. "But there are children! That's not right! Why are there children in The Periphery?"

"People make children, Heart. The people in The Periphery are free to live their lives as they choose. People used to be put in prisons. That punishment was so much worse than now. In these days, we are humane. People who act against society are simply removed from society and its advantages," Keeper D preached. "The Wall keeps them from entering where we live, and from having the numerous advantages of harnessed Dark Energy.

"You wouldn't have us take the children from their mothers and fathers, would you? If they choose to have children, those children, too, live in The Periphery. It's not so bad for them. They don't know what they've never had." Keeper D moved pointedly away from Heart, taking up the hands of two of the other Darling Undesirables. "Let's continue with our tour, shall we? Our docent had been very patient with us."

"Oh, that's all right," the docent began, " I don't m ...."

"Still," Keeper D interrupted, "I think it best that we keep moving. The children are restless. Other people are here as well, wanting to see the exhibits. I'm sure we've kept this wing closed more than long enough." She moved down the hall swiftly, with the feet of the two Darling Undesirables in her grip pedaling rapidly to try to match her long stride.

"We'd better keep up with her," the docent said, herding the rest of the group, while Heart took Eye's hand in her own.

"Such a lot ...." he said.

"Going on," she completed.

"Yes."

Heart thought she would never have anything as big and terrible to think about as those children in The Periphery. Not like she was, and Eye, and all the other Darling Undesirables, who had no parents, who were just faulty test tube experiments, but lived a life of luxury. Those sad, real, young people living in darkness and cold and hunger, hurt her in a deep, sacred place.

But she didn't know what would soon befall her.

DEAR READER ....

Thank you for reading *The Heart of Leo*.

Don't miss any of Heart's saga!

The Darling Undesirables, Moons Rising, The Inventor's Clone, Heart's Quest, and ***The Heart of Leo*** are available wherever books are sold.

To see a different side of my work, you may enter the following web address for a gift of e-posters from my book, ***Life Flows on the River of Love:***

http://eepurl.com/cKLPxn

About the Author

I live in a forest in the Pacific Northwest with a few domestic and numerous wild creatures, where I create an ever-growing inventory of books and stories.

When you support my work you help support ten acres of natural forest, and all its resident fauna. *All the creatures and I thank you!*

Questions, comments, observations, reviews? I'd love to hear from you!:

Blythe@BlytheAyne.com

www.BlytheAyne.com

www.ingramcontent.com/pod-product-compliance
Lightning Source LLC
Chambersburg PA
CBHW071817190726
48292CB00008B/2885